Bluey

FOR REAL LIFE
A STORY COLLECTION

PENGUIN YOUNG READERS LICENSES
An imprint of Penguin Random House LLC, New York

The stories in this book were originally published individually as follows:

First published in Australia by Puffin Books as *The Beach* in 2019, *Bob Bilby* in 2020,
The Creek in 2020, and *Fruit Bat* in 2019

First published in the United States of America by Penguin Young Readers Licenses as *The Beach* in 2021,
Bob Bilby in 2021, *The Creek* in 2020, and *Good Night, Fruit Bat* in 2020

This bind-up edition first published in the United States of America by Penguin Young Readers Licenses,
an imprint of Penguin Random House LLC, New York, 2021

This book is based on the TV series *Bluey*.

BLUEY™ and BLUEY character logos ™ & © Ludo Studio Pty Ltd 2018.
Licensed by BBC Studios. BBC logo ™ & © BBC 1996.

Visit us online at penguinrandomhouse.com.

Manufactured in China

ISBN 9780593386842   10 9 8 7 6 5 4 HH

TABLE OF CONTENTS

Good Night, Fruit Bat 1

The Creek 25

Bob Bilby 49

The Beach 73

Meet the Characters 97

BLUEY

GOOD NIGHT, FRUIT BAT

Bluey, Bingo, Mum, and Dad are playing pop-up croc.

"AGAIN!" says Bluey, when the game ends.

"No, that's it. Bedtime," Mum replies.

Not fair. Bluey doesn't want to go to bed.

"All right," says Dad, following Bluey and Bingo outside.
"Say good night to the animals."

Bingo waves. "Night, kangaroos. Night, bilbies."

"Night, fruit bats," says Dad.

"No, fruit bats don't sleep at night.
They're 'octurnal,'" explains Bingo.

"You mean they don't need to go to bed now?" asks Bluey.

"No, but you do," says Dad.

Bluey wishes she was a **FRUIT BAT**.

But **FRUIT BATS** don't get to play rocket ship! Dad zooms Bluey and Bingo upstairs to the bathroom.

"I don't need a shower," complains Bluey.

"Yeah, you do, ya grub," says Dad.

"Not fair. I bet **FRUIT BATS** don't have to have showers," says Bluey.

POAHH!

But **FRUIT BATS** don't get to play penguins!

"Look at me, Mum!" says Bluey.

And they don't get to play the story game.

Dad starts reading. "She opened the door, but out jumped a huge . . . hairy . . ."

"... *snore!*"

zzzzzzz

"WAKE UP!" the kids squeal.

"...SPIDER!" Dad yells.

They laugh until Mum comes in and kisses them good night.

Not fair. Bluey wants to be a **FRUIT BAT**, not go to bed.

Bluey sneaks downstairs and cheekily asks Mum if she can stay up.

Dad is asleep on the floor, dreaming about playing touch footy.

"He doesn't get to play much anymore," Mum explains.

"Why doesn't he get to play it for real life?" asks Bluey.

"He's busy, sweetheart, working and looking after you two."

That doesn't seem very fair.

Bluey has an idea.
If Dad dreams about footy,
maybe she can dream about
being a **FRUIT BAT**. She
runs back up to bed.

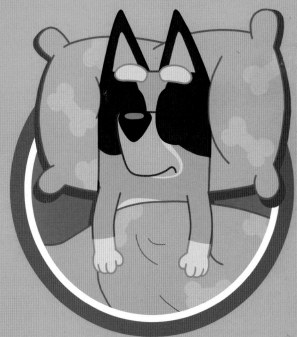

Bluey closes her eyes and all of a sudden she's soaring high above their house, flapping her arms like a **FRUIT BAT**.

She flies past bedroom windows and sees Mackenzie fast asleep.

She gets massively full
eating lots of fruit.

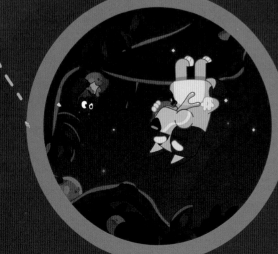

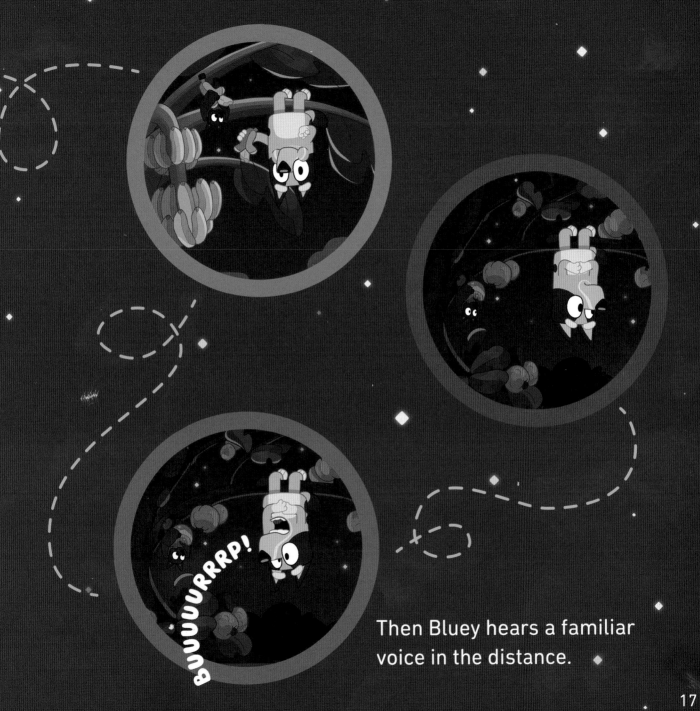

Then Bluey hears a familiar
voice in the distance.

It's Dad playing footy with his mates.

"**HEY, DAD!**" yells Bluey.

"Hey, Bluey! You're a **FRUIT BAT!**" says Dad, waving. "How is it?"

"It's great," says Bluey. "You get to eat a lot of fruit."

19

It looks like Dad is having a lot of fun
playing footy. No wonder he misses it.

It's time to head home.

When Bluey wakes up the next morning, she thinks
about Dad. It doesn't seem fair that he doesn't get
to play footy for real life.

But she's never heard him whine about it. Not even once.

"I had the most amazing dream," Bluey says, walking into the kitchen for breakfast.

Dad's doing sit-ups, so he's ready for when he plays footy again one day. Bluey has something to tell him . . .

"Thanks for looking after us, Dad," Bluey says,
giving him a hug.

"YOU'RE WELCOME."

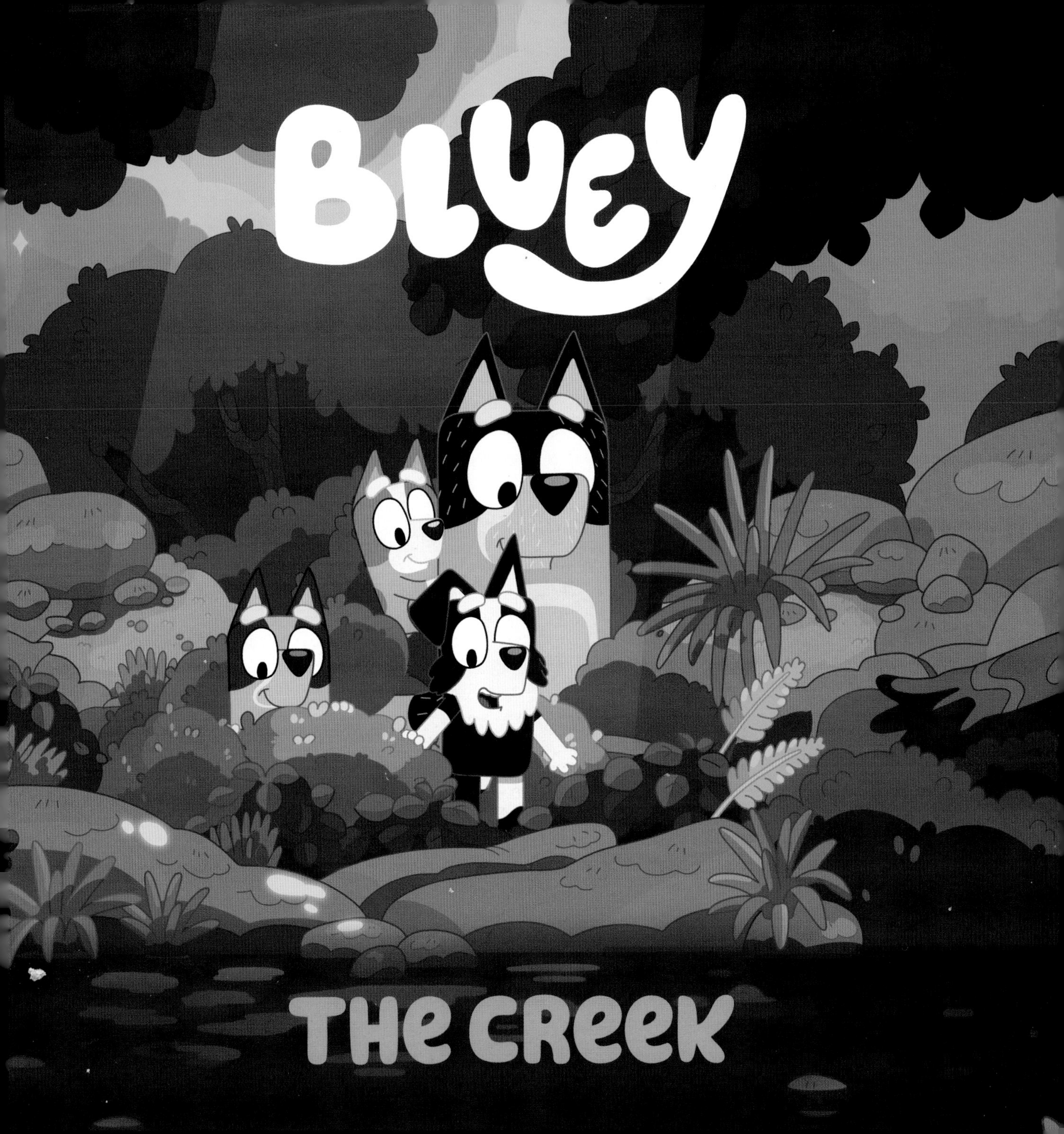
BLUEY
THE CREEK

Bluey's bored of the playground.
She's played on everything twice.

Mackenzie has an idea.
"What about we go to
the creek?"

"Yeah, I'll take you down to the creek," says Dad.

27

"YAYYY!" cry the kids.

Dad scoops up Bingo and races off. "Let's bush bash!"

Bluey holds back. She's not sure what the creek is like.
Maybe she might just stay in the playground . . .

But Mackenzie won't let her. "C'mon, Bluey!

The creek is very different from the playground.

There are more thorns here.

More spiders . . .

. . . and **DEFINITELY** more leeches!

31

But there's also more of these fellas.

The gang heads down a slope. The ground is more uneven here. And there are no steps like at the playground!

AGHHHHHHHHHHH!

"Wow," says Bingo when they arrive at the creek.
Both Mackenzie and Bingo think **THE CREEK IS BEAUTIFUL**.
But Bluey still wonders if they're right.

Dad and Bingo lead them to the spot where he played as a kid. They rock hop across the water.

Some of the rocks are pointy. Others are wobbly.

And the green ones are slippery!

"It's so lovely."

"THE CREEK IS BEAUTIFUL,"
Bluey says to herself.

"Woooh!"

"I'm not scared of it at all."
But she might be a little.

Bluey is getting the hang of the creek!

"You made it, Squirt!" says Dad.

The creek is an adventure.

"Here we are! I don't think I've been to the creek since I was your age," says Dad. "It still looks the same."

The creek must be really old then.

40

Bluey's not sure what to play. In the playground it is easy. But the creek is different.

Just then
a dragonfly
flutters past.

And Bluey just starts
mucking around.

Skipping stones . . .

. . . and making boats.

And building dams.

Bluey thinks the creek is fun.

At Daddy Day Spa, Dad finally gets his nails done.

Bingo slops a mud pack on Dad. "This will make you very beautiful. Oh, I'm out of mud!"

"I'll get some more," volunteers Bluey and heads off.

Bluey squelches her paws into the mud.
Suddenly, there's a rustling noise.
Bluey looks up and gasps.

A potoroo!

They stare at each other, the potoroo's
nose twitching before it bounds off.

As the gang heads home,
Bluey doesn't have to wonder
if Mackenzie and Bingo were right.
She knows for sure,
deep inside . . .

. . . that **THE CREEK IS BEAUTIFUL**.

Hi, my name is Bob. I'm a bilby. I like making new **FRIENDS** and having **FUN TIMES** with them. Like most bilbies, I'm not much of a talker.

Today I'm going home with Bingo Heeler. She seems really nice. I'm already **FRIENDS** with her sister, Bluey.

I wonder what we'll get up to.

At Bingo's house, I show her family my book. It has photos of all the adventures I've had with my **FRIENDS**.

This is Jasper W.
He likes Australian rules
football.

This is me on a trip
with Mrs. Terrier. It was
cold in Scotland.

Look at my yellow
karate belt here!

Every new **FRIEND** has
their own way to have
FUN TIMES.

"Oh, you did a bit of karate, Bob," says Bingo's mum. "Wackadoo!"

I sure did! I learned it when I stayed with my **FRIEND** Maxie.

HEE-YA!

Bingo's ready to show me how she has **FUN TIMES**.
But first, that sausage roll the big blue guy has looks yum.

55

We play Moo Cow, and Bluey and Bingo show me the tablet. I've never seen one before. It can take photos.

CLICK!

moo!

57

We watch cartoons on the way to the shops. I love watching cartoons. The cartoon characters have so much fun.

"Don't you want to teach Bob some car games?"
asks Bingo's mum.

Maybe after the cartoons are finished.

At the shops, we watch even more cartoons on an even bigger tablet! So many pretty colors.

Bingo's mum watches hockey on the big tablets, too.
I love hockey. I wonder if Bingo and I will play hockey
when we get home.

We don't. We watch more cartoons. I think I'm ready to do something else with Bingo now. Our time together is almost over.

"Kids, I'm putting our photos in Bob Bilby's book,"
calls Bingo's mum. She's been taking photos all day.

But when Bingo looks at the book, she sees the photos are all just of me watching cartoons. Bingo gets upset.

Bluey seems to understand. "Bob just copies everything we do, and all we're doing is really **BORING** stuff. So we need to do some really **EXCITING** stuff instead!"

She takes all their tablets and puts them in a basket.

Bingo's mum gets out the bikes.
Bingo and I are about to have **FUN TIMES**!

The big blue guy takes photos of our adventures.

We play at the park and get
dizzy going round and round.

We ride on Sparklemane
and pretend she can fly.

67

The fireworks are my favorite thing ever.
So many pretty colors.
I love my **FRIEND** Bingo.

68

Back at kindergarten, Bingo and I tell the class about our **FUN
TIMES** together and show them the new photos in my book.

Then it's time for me to have an adventure with Missy.
I'm going to miss Bingo.

I hope she knows how happy I am that we're **FRIENDS**.

She seems
upset again.

I want to tell Bingo that I had
so much fun with her, and I
can't wait to see her again.

But I'm not much of a talker.

BLUEY

 THE BEACH

Bluey, Bingo, Mum, and Dad are off to the beach.

They set up the tent, roll around in the sand, and then race to the water.

Bluey and Bingo pretend the waves are trying to splash them.

Here comes a **BIG** one!

Mum is off for a walk along the beach.

"Why do you like walking by yourself?" asks Bluey.

"I'm not sure," says Mum. "**I JUST DO.** See you soon, little mermaid."

What a strange answer, thinks Bluey.

Not long after, she finds a beautiful shell and asks to show Mum.

"All right, off you go," says Dad.

"FOR REAL LIFE?" says Bluey. "All by myself?"

Dad nods. "Just don't go in the water."

Bingo waves her hands over Bluey's tail.
Bluey laughs. "I am the mermaid who got her **LEGS!**"

Mum is now a tiny orange speck.

"Hmmm." Bluey frowns. "Maybe I'll just stay here with you and Dad."

"But, little mermaid, you can follow Mum's footsteps," says Bingo.

"OH YEAH!" Bluey grins. "Thanks!"

Bluey **HOPS** from one footprint to another.
She **RUNS** and **SKIPS** and does **CARTWHEELS**
in the sand until . . .

. . . she comes across a flock of seagulls.

"Um, can you **PLEASE** move?" Bluey asks politely.

It's a good thing mermaids aren't scared of seagulls!

RUFF!
RUFF!

Bluey laughs as she **HOPS** from one footprint to another.
She **RUNS** and **SKIPS** and does **CARTWHEELS**
in the sand until . . .

. . . a **BIG** wave sneaks up and **CRASHES** onto the shore. It takes Mum's footsteps out to sea.

"Ooh, you **CHEEKY** wave!" Bluey barks. "How will I find Mum now?"

Just as Bluey begins to lose hope, she spots a pipi coming up for **wee-wees!**

HEE-HEE HEE-HEE

PINCHY! PINCHY!

A crab scuttles past.

Bluey copies its funny sideways walk.

"**Ha-Ha!** I am the mermaid who got her **CRAB LEGS!**"

AARGH!

Bluey scampers away.

. . . then **SKIDS** to a stop.
"A jellyfish! How will
I get past?"

She **RUNS** and **RUNS** . . .

She picks up a stick and pokes the blue blob. It wobbles hello.

"Ha-ha! You can't sting me, jellyfish! **I AM THE MERMAID WHO GOT HER LEGS, BUT ONLY FOR A DAY!**"

Bluey races ahead.

"Look at this amazing shell!"
she calls, but Mum's still
too far away to hear.

Better keep going!

MUM!

Bluey **RUNS** and **SKIPS** and does **CARTWHEELS** in the sand until she comes across an old castle.

Perhaps this is where all the other mermaids lived, she thinks, and leaves her stick as a present.

Then she slowly backs away and bumps right into . . .

. . . a pelican!

Bluey begins to think she's had enough of walking by herself . . .

She looks back at Dad, but he's just a tiny blue speck.

"If I can't go backwards, and I can't go forwards, what am I going to do?"

Bluey remembers the seagulls and the crabs and the jellyfish. If she got past them, maybe she can get past a pelican, too . . .

She summons every bit of courage. After all, a little mermaid has got to be brave.

I am the mermaid who got her legs, but only for a day!

Then she tiptoes around
the pelican.

The pelican beats his great big wings and flies away.

THANK YOU FOR MOVING, MR. PELICAN!

A familiar voice floats towards Bluey.
She gasps and spins around.

Bluey holds the shell to Mum's ear. It has the whole beach inside it.

Bluey and Mum head back together.

"I **LOVE** walking by myself," says Bluey.

"Oh yeah, why's that?" asks Mum.

Bluey thinks. That's a hard question. "I don't know, **I JUST DO**."

MEET THE CHARACTERS

BLUEY

BLUEY is a six-year-old blue heeler who loves to play and is very good at inventing games with her friends and her little sister, Bingo. Her favorite games are when she pretends to be a grown-up doing grown-up things. Like being a dancing granny, a bad taxi driver, or even a backpack!

When things don't go the way Bluey planned, she will let everyone know. But she is slowly learning that sometimes what really matters is to just go with the flow.

BINGO

BINGO is Bluey's little sister. She is a ball of energy. When she's not playing, you can find her daydreaming or relaxing in her relaxer chair.

She loves playing with Bluey, but sometimes she has to find her big girl bark to stand up for herself.

BANDIT

BANDIT is Bluey and Bingo's dad. He loves to play with them and is often involved in their games. He can be an angry octopus, a horse, a sick patient, or even Santa!

When he's not playing, he works as an archaeologist. He also enjoys playing footy and going to the pool!

CHILLI

CHILLI is Bluey and Bingo's mum. She juggles working at Airport Security, raising her two children, playing hockey, and catching up with her friends.

She is a good listener who always knows what to say and tells the best stories. She sees the funny side of everything and loves to join in with the family games.

MUFFIN is Bluey and Bingo's nonstop cousin. Muffin loves to talk and play, but she can get a little overexcited at times.

AUNT TRIXIE is Muffin and Socks's mum. She likes to play hockey with Chilli.

SOCKS

SOCKS is Muffin's little sister who's still learning how to walk and talk! Socks might be too young to learn all the rules, but she and Bluey always know how to have a good time.

UNCLE STRIPE

UNCLE STRIPE is Bandit's good-natured younger brother and Muffin and Socks's dad. Like Bandit, he's always up for some kind of sport, but he's just as happy lying on the couch watching telly.

Nana

Nana is Bandit's mum, and she's not too old to learn new tricks—like flossing! She's always got time to chat to Bluey and Bingo on the tablet and hear all their news.

Grandad

Grandad is Chilli's dad. He lives off the grid, outside of the city. He loves to play with Bluey and Bingo and take them on adventures in the bush—even when he should be resting!

MACKENZIE

MACKENZIE loves to play with all his friends and think outside the box as a spy or a lion tamer! He likes to race barky boats with Bluey.

SNICKERS

SNICKERS loves the stars and machines. He isn't the fastest runner in the pack, but he's always got great ideas for new games to play.

COCO

COCO doesn't always follow the rules, but she loves to play with everyone! She's the youngest of eight siblings!

RUSTY

RUSTY already knows how to ride a mini-motorbike, and his favorite game is playing Mums and Dads with Indy.

CHLOE

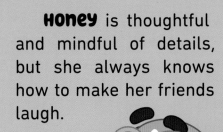

CHLOE's favorite game is playing Adventure. Soft-spoken, kind, and gentle, she is a good friend to Bluey.

HONEY is thoughtful and mindful of details, but she always knows how to make her friends laugh.

HONEY

INDY

INDY is very creative and open to try anything! She can't eat wheat, gluten, sugar, dairy, or food with added ingredients.

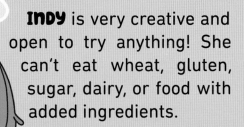

LUCKY

LUCKY is Bluey and Bingo's next-door neighbor. He loves sports and is always kicking a footy around the backyard or watching cricket with his dad.

JUDO

JUDO is Bluey and Bingo's next-door neighbor. She often hops over the fence to play with them and likes to be the leader in lots of games.

Jean LUC met Bluey while camping. He and his family are French Canadian and only speak French, but he and Bluey enjoy playing together, anyway.

Jean LUC

THE TERRIERS are unstoppable forces of nature! They are here to defend you!

THE TERRIERS

MISSY

MISSY is one of Bingo's friends from Kindy. She's pretty small, which sometimes makes her afraid, but when her friends need her help she can be super brave!